I0621125

THE BARBARIANS

Start Publishing PD LLC
Copyright © 2024 by Start Publishing PD LLC

All rights reserved, including the right to reproduce this book or portions thereof in any form whatsoever.

Start Publishing PD is a registered trademark of Start Publishing PD LLC
Manufactured in the United States of America

Cover art: Shutterstock/Taisiya Kozorez

Cover design: Jennifer Do

10 9 8 7 6 5 4 3 2 1

ISBN 979-8-8809-1320-6

THE BARBARIANS

by Algis Budrys

History was repeating itself; there were moats and nobles in Pennsylvania and vassals in Manhattan and the barbarian hordes were overrunning the land.

It was just as he saw The Barbarian's squat black tankette lurch hurriedly into a nest of boulders that young Giulion Geoffrey realized he had been betrayed. With the muzzle of his own cannon still hot from the shell that had jammed The Barbarian's turret, he had yanked the starboard track lever to wheel into position for the finishing shot. All around him, the remnants of The Barbarian's invading army were being cut to flaming ribbons by the armored vehicles of the Seaboard League. The night was shot through by billows of cannon fire, and the din of laboring engines, guns, and rent metal was a cacophonic climax to the Seaboard League's first decisive victory over the inland invaders. Young Geoffrey could justifiably feel that he would cap that climax by personally accounting for the greatest of the inland barbarians; the barbarian general himself. He trained his sights on the scarlet bearpaw painted on the skewed turret's flank, and laid his hand on the firing lever.

Out of the corner of his eye, he caught a glimpse of another tankette rushing up on his port side. He glanced at it, saw its graceful handcrafting, and knew it for one of the League's own. He could even see the insigne; the mailed heel trampling a stand of wheat; Harolde Dugald, of the neighboring fief. Geoffrey was on coldly polite terms with Dugald—he had no use for the other man's way of treating his serfs—and now he felt a prickle of indignant rage at this attempt to usurp a share of his glory. He saw Dugald's turret begin to traverse, and hastily tried to get the finishing shot into The Barbarian's tankette before the other Leaguesman could fire. But

THE BARBARIANS

Dugald was not aiming for The Barbarian. First he had to eliminate Geoffrey from the scene entirely. When he fired, at almost point-blank range, the world seemed to explode in Giulion's eyes.

Somehow, no whistling shard of metal actually hit him. But the tankette, sturdy as it was, could not hope to protect him entirely. He was thrown viciously into the air, his ribs first smashing into the side of the hatch, and then he was thrown clear, onto the rocky ground of the foothills; agonized, stunned to semi-consciousness, he lay feebly beating at his smoldering tunic while Dugald spun viciously by him, almost crushing him under one tread. He saw Dugald's tankette plunge into the rocks after The Barbarian, and then, suddenly, the battle was beyond him. Dugald, The Barbarian; all the thundering might that had clashed here on the eastern seaboard of what had, long ago, been The United States of America—all of this had suddenly, as battles will, whirled off in a new direction and left Giulion Geoffrey to lie hurt and unconscious in the night.

*

He awoke to the trickle of cold water between his teeth. His lips bit into the threaded metal of a canteen top, and a huge arm supported his shoulders. Broad shoulders and a massive head loomed over him against the stars. A rumbling, gentle voice said: "All right, lad, now swallow some before it's all wasted."

He peered around him in the night. It was as still as the bottom of a grave. Nothing moved. He drew a ragged breath that ended in a sharp gasp, and the rumbling voice said: "Ribs?"

He nodded and managed a strangled "Yes."

"Shouldn't wonder," the stranger grunted. "I saw you pop out of your tank like a cork coming out of a wine bottle. That was a fair shot he hit you. You're lucky." A broad hand pressed him down as the memory of Dugald's treachery started him struggling to his feet.

"Hold still, lad. We'll give you a chance to catch your breath and wrap some bandages around you. You'll live to give him his due, but not tonight. You'll have to wait for another day."

There was something in the stranger's voice that Geoffrey recognized for the quality that made men obey other men. It was competence, self-assurance, and, even more, the calm expression of good sense. Tonight, Geoffrey needed someone with that quality. He sank back, grateful for the stranger's help. "I'm Giulion Geoffrey of Geoffrion," he said, "and indebted to you. Who are you, stranger?"

The darkness rumbled to a deep, rueful laugh. "In these parts, lad, I'm not called by my proper name. I'm Hodd Savage—The Barbarian. And that was a fair knock *you* gave *me*."

Young Geoffrey's silence lasted for a long while. Then he said in a flat, distant voice: "Why did you give me water, if you're going to kill me anyway?"

The Barbarian laughed again, this time in pure amusement. "Because I'm not going to kill you, obviously. You're too good a cannoneer to be despatched by a belt knife. No—no, lad, I'm not planning to kill anyone for some time. All I want right now is to get out of here and get home. I've got another army to raise, to make up for this pasting you Leaguesmen have just given me."

"Next time, you won't be so lucky," Geoffrey muttered. "We'll see your hide flapping in the rain, if you're ever foolish enough to raid our lands again."

The Barbarian slapped his thigh. "By God," he chuckled, "I knew it wasn't some ordinary veal-fed princeling that outmaneuvered *me*!" He shook his head. "That other pup had better watch out for you, if you ever cross his path again. I lost him in the rocks with ease to spare. Bad luck your shot smashed my fuel tanks, or I'd be halfway home by now." The rolling voice grew low and bitter. "No sense waiting to pick up my men. Not enough of 'em left to make a corporal's guard."

"What do you mean, *if* I ever cross Dugald's path again? I'll have him called out to trial by combat the day I can ride a tankette once more."

"I wouldn't be too sure, lad," The Barbarian said gently. "What does that look like, over there?"

Geoffrey turned his head to follow the shadowy pointing arm, and saw a flicker of light in the distance. He recognized it for what it was; a huge campfire, with the Leaguesmen's tankettes drawn up around it. "They're dividing the spoils—what prisoners there are, to work the mills; whatever of your equipment is still usable; your baggage train. And so forth. What of it?"

"Ah, yes, my baggage train," The Barbarian muttered. "Well, we'll come back to that. What else do you suppose they're dividing?"

Geoffrey frowned. "Why—nothing else. Wait!" He sat up sharply, ignoring his ribs. "The fiefs of the dead nobles."

"Exactly. Your ramshackle little League held together long enough to whip us for the first time, but now the princelings are dividing up and returning to their separate holdings. Once there, they'll go back to peering covetously at each other's lands, and maybe raid amongst themselves a little, until I come back again. And you're as poor as a church mouse at this moment, lad—no fief, no lands, no title—unless there's an heir?"

Geoffrey shook his head distractedly. "No. I've not wed. It's as you say."

"And just try to get your property back. No—no, it won't be so easy to return. Unless you'd care to be a serf on your own former holding?"

"Dugald would have me killed," Geoffrey said bitterly.

"So there you are, lad. The only advantage you have is that Dugald thinks you're dead already—you can be sure of that, or it would have been an assassin, and not me, that woke you. That's something, at least. It's a beginning, but you'll have to lay your plans carefully, and take your time. I certainly wouldn't plan on doing anything until your body's healed and your brain's had time to work."

Young Geoffrey blinked back the tears of rage. The thought of losing the town and lands his father had left him was almost more than his hot blood could stand. The memory of the great old Keep that dominated the town, with its tapestried halls and torchlit chambers, was suddenly very precious to him. He felt a sharp pang at the thought that he must sleep in a field tonight, like some skulking outlaw, while Dugald quite possibly got himself drunk on Geoffrion wine and snored his headache away on the thick furs of Geoffrey's bed.

But The Barbarian was right. Time was needed—and this meant that, to a certain extent at least, his lot and Savage's were thrown in together. The thought came to Geoffrey that he might have chosen a worse partner.

"Now, lad," The Barbarian said, "as long as you're not doing anything else, you might as well help me with my problem."

The realization of just exactly who this man was came sharply back to young Geoffrey. "I won't help you escape to your own lands, if that's what you mean," he said quickly.

"I'll take good care of that myself, when the time comes," the man answered drily. "Right now, I've got something else in mind. They're dividing my baggage train, as you said. Now, I don't mind that, seeing as most of it belonged to them in the first place. I don't mind it for this year, that is. But there's something else one of you cockerels will be wanting to take home with him, and I've a mind not to let him.

THE BARBARIANS

There's a perfectly good woman in my personal trailer, and I'm going to get her. But if we're going to do that and get clear of this country by morning, we'd better get to it."

Like every other young man of his time and place, Geoffrey had a clear-cut sense of duty regarding the safety and well-being of ladies. He had an entirely different set of attitudes toward women who were not ladies. He had not the slightest idea of which to apply to this case.

What sort of woman would The Barbarian take to battle with him? What sort of women would the inland barbarians have generally? He had very little knowledge to go on. The inlanders had been appearing from over the westward mountains for generations, looting and pillaging almost at will, sometimes staying through a winter but usually disappearing in the early Fall, carrying their spoils back to their mysterious homelands on the great Mississippi plain. The seaboard civilization had somehow kept from going to its knees, in spite of them—in this last generation, even though the barbarians had The Barbarian to lead them, the Seaboard League had managed to cobble itself together—but no one, in all this time, had ever actually learned, or cared, much about these vicious, compactly organized raiders. Certainly no one had learned anything beyond those facts which worked to best advantage on a battlefield.

So, young Giulion Geoffrey faced his problem. This 'perfectly good woman' of The Barbarian's—was she in fact a good woman, a lady, and therefore entitled to aid in extremity from any and all gentlemen; or was she some camp follower, entirely worthy of being considered a spoil of combat?

"Well, come on, lad," The Barbarian rumbled impatiently at this point. "Do you want that Dugald enjoying *her* tonight along with everything else?"

And that decided Geoffrey. He pushed himself to his feet, not liking the daggers in his chest, but not liking the thought of Dugald's pleasures even more. "Let's go, then."

"Good enough, lad," The Barbarian chuckled. "Now let's see how quietly we can get across to the edge of that fire."

They set out—none too quietly, with The Barbarian's heavy bulk lurching against Geoffrey's lean shoulder on occasion, and both of them uncertain of their footing in the darkness. But they made it across without being noticed—just two more battle-sore figures in a field where many such might be expected—and that was what counted.

The noise and confusion attendant on the dividing of the spoils was an added help; they reached the fringes of the campfire easily.

*

It was very interesting, the way history had doubled back on itself, like a worm re-growing part of its body but re-growing it in the wrong place. At one end of the kink—of the fresh, pink scar—was a purulent hell of fire and smoke that no one might have expected to live through. Yet, people had, as they have a habit of doing. And at the other end of the kink in time—Giulion Geoffrey's end, Harolde Dugald's time, The Barbarian's day—there were keeps and moats in Erie, Pennsylvania, vassals in New Brunswick, and a great stinking warren of low, half-timbered houses on the island of Manhattan. If it had taken a few centuries longer to recover from the cauterizing sun bombs, these things might still have been. But they might have had different names, and human history might have been considered to begin only a few hundred years before. Even this had not happened. The link with the past remained. There was a narrow, cobbled path on Manhattan, with sewage oozing down the ditch in its center, which was still Fifth Avenue. It ran roughly along the same

11

directions as old Broadway, not because there was no one who could read the yellowed old maps but because surveying was in its second childhood. There was a barge running between two ropes stretched across the Hudson, and this was The George Washington Bridge ferry. So, it was only a kink in history, not a break.

But Rome was not re-built in a day. Hodd Savage—The Barbarian, the man who had come out of the hinterlands to batter on civilization's badly mortared walls—clamped his hand on Giulion Geoffrey's arm, grunted, jerked his head toward the cluster of nobles standing beside the campfire, and muttered: "Listen."

Geoffrey listened.

The nobles were between him and the fire, and almost none of them were more than silhouettes. Here and there, a man faced toward the fire at such an angle that Geoffrey could make out the thick arch of an eyebrow, the jut of a cheek, or the crook of a nose. But it was not enough for recognition. All the nobles were dressed in battle accoutrements that had become stained or torn. Their harness had shifted, their tunics were askew, and they were bunched so closely that the outline of one man blended into the mis-shaped shadow of the next. The voices were hoarse from an afternoon's bellowing. Some were still drunk with the acid fire of exhausted nerves, and were loud. Others, drained, mumbled in the background like a chorus of the stupid. Gesticulating, mumbling, shouting, shadowed, lumped into one knot of blackness lighted by a ruddy cheekbone here, a gleaming brow there above an eye socket as inky and blank as a bottomless pit, they were like something out of the wan and misty ages before the Earth had had time to form completely.

Two arguing voices rose out of the mass:

"Those three barbarian tankettes are *mine*, I say!"

"Yours when I lie dead!"

"They surrendered to me!"

"Because I pounded them into submission."

"Into submission, indeed! You skulked around their flanks like a lame dog, and now that I've taken them, you want your bone!"

"You were glad enough to see me there when the battle was hot. Call me a dog again and I'll spit you like a rat on a pitchfork."

No one else in the group of nobles paid the two of them any attention. No one had time to spare for any quarrel but his own, and the whole squabbling pile of them looked ready to fly apart at any moment—to draw sidearms and knives and flare into spiteful combat.

The Barbarian spat quietly. "There's your Seaboard League, lad. There's your convocation of free men. Step out there and ask for your lands back. Care to try?"

"We've already decided that wouldn't be wise," Geoffrey said irritably. He had never cared much for these inevitable aftermaths to battle, but it made him angry to have an inland barbarian make pointed comments. "I suppose it's different when *you* win, eh?"

"Not very. But then, we're not civilized. Let's get moving, lad."

Silently, they skirted the fire and made their way toward the parked vehicles of The Barbarian's captured supply train. The ground was rough and covered by underbrush. More than once, The Barbarian stumbled into Geoffrey, making him clench his jaw against the pain in his chest. But he saw no point in saying anything about it.

"There she is," The Barbarian said in a husky growl. Geoffrey peered through the brush at an armored trailer whose flat sides were completely undecorated except for a scarlet bearpaw painted on the door. A lantern gleamed behind the slit windows, and The Barbarian grunted with satisfaction. "She's still in there. Fine. We'll have this done in a couple of seconds."

13

THE BARBARIANS

In spite of the incongruity, Geoffrey asked curiously: "What's a second?"

"A division of time, lad—one sixtieth of a minute."

"Oh. What on Earth would you want to measure that accurately for?"

"For getting women out of trailers in a hurry, lad. Now—let's look for sentries."

There were two guarding the trailer—men-at-arms from Dugald's holding, Geoffrey noticed—carrying shotguns and lounging in the shadows. One of them had a wineskin—Geoffrey heard the gurgle plainly—and the other was constantly turning away from the trailer to listen to the shrieks and shouting coming from among the other vehicles of the train, where other guards were not being quite as careful of their masters' new property.

"I see they've found the quartermaster's waggons," The Barbarian said drily. "Now, then, lad—you work away toward the right, there, and I'll take the left. Here—take my knife. I won't need it." The Barbarian passed over a length of steel as big as a short-sword, but oddly curved and sharpened down one side of the blade. "Stab if you can, but if you have to cut, that blade'll go through a man's forearm. Remember you're not holding one of those overgrown daggers of yours."

"And just why should I kill a man for you?"

"Do you think that man won't try to kill you?"

Geoffrey had no satisfactory answer to that. He moved abruptly off into the brush, holding The Barbarian's knife, and wondering just how far he was obligated for a bandaged chest and half a pint of water. But a man's duty to his rescuer was plain enough, and, besides, just what else was there to do?

The blame for it all went squarely back to Dugald, and Geoffrey did not love him for it. He slipped through the bushes until he was only a few yards from the man who had the wineskin, and waited for The Barbarian to appear at the opposite end of the trailer.

When it happened, it happened quite suddenly, as these things will. One moment the other sentry was craning his neck for another look at what was going on elsewhere. The next he was down on his knees, croaking through a compressed throat, with The Barbarian's arm under his chin and a driving knee ready to smash at the back of his neck again.

Geoffrey jumped forward, toward his own man. The man-at-arms had dropped his wineskin in surprise and was staring at what was happening to his comrade. When he heard Geoffrey come out of the underbrush, the face he turned was white and oddly distended with shock, as though all the bones had drained out of it. He might have appeared fierce enough, ordinarily. But things were happening too fast for him.

Geoffrey had never killed anyone but a noble in his life. Not intentionally and at close range, in any case. The completely baffled and helpless look of this one somehow found time to remind him that this was not, after all, one of his peers—that the man was hopelessly outclassed in fair combat—or in anything else, for that matter. Geoffrey did *not* stop to weigh the probity of this idea. It was the central tenet of his education and environment. Furthermore, there was some truth in it.

He couldn't kill the man. He swept up his arm and struck the flat of The Barbarian's broad knife against the side of the guard's head, and bowled the man over with his rush. But the guard had a hard skull. He stared up with glazed but conscious eyes, and squalled: "Lord Geoffrey!" Geoffrey hit him again, and this time the guard

15

stayed down, but the damage was done. Scrambling to his feet, Geoffrey ran over to The Barbarian, who was letting the other guard ooze to the ground.

"We'll have to hurry!" Geoffrey panted. "Before that man comes back to his senses."

The Barbarian gave him a disgusted look, but nodded. "Hurry we shall." He lurched to the trailer door and slapped it with the flat of his hand. "Let's go, Myka."

There was a scrambling sound inside the trailer, and the light went out. The door slid open, and Geoffrey found himself staring at the most beautiful woman he had ever seen.

She was lithe almost to the point of boyishness, even though she was clearly some years older than Geoffrey. She had short hair the color of hammered copper, high cheekbones, and tawny eyes. She was wearing a tunic and short trousers, and there was an empty pistol holster strapped around her waist. Obviously, she was not a lady. But it was much too late for Geoffrey to care about that. She stopped in the doorway, shaking her head slowly at The Barbarian. "I swear, Hodd," she said in a low, laughing voice, "one of these days you *won't* come back from the dead, and I'll be surprised."

"It was close enough, this time," The Barbarian growled. He jerked his head toward Geoffrey. "That young buck over there knows how to handle his enemies. Once he learns what to do about his friends, I may have to retire."

Myka arched her burning eyebrows. "Oh? What's the story behind that, I'd like to know."

"We can always talk," Geoffrey said a little edgily. "But we can't always find an empty tankette."

"Quite right, lad," The Barbarian said. "I saw some vehicles parked over that way."

"Those belong to the nobles. There ought to be some captured ones of yours somewhere around here."

"With plenty of guards on them. No, thanks."

"That didn't trouble you earlier."

"Myka, as you may have noticed, is more than a tank. This time the prize isn't worth it. I'd rather just slip over to where I can get transportation for the choosing."

"Not with my help."

The Barbarian looked at him and grunted. He seemed oddly disappointed. "I would have bet the other way," he muttered. Then the shaggy head rose, and he circled Myka's waist with one arm. "All right, I'll do it without your help."

"Is Myka trained to drive a tankette and fight at the same time?"

"No."

"Then you'd better do it my way. You'd make a poor showing, kicking drive levers with a broken leg." Geoffrey nodded toward The Barbarian's right shin. "It's been that way since before you picked me up, hasn't it? I saw it wobble when you kneed that man-at-arms."

Myka looked at The Barbarian sharply, worry on her face, but the man was chuckling. "All right, bucko, we'll do it your way."

"Fine." Geoffrey wasn't so sure it was. Suddenly he was committed not only to helping The Barbarian escape, but also to escape with him. He was faintly surprised at himself. But there was something about the man. Something worth saving, no matter what. And there was the business now of having been recognized. Once Dugald learned he was still alive, there would be a considerable amount of danger in staying in the vicinity. Of course, he had only to stoop over the unconscious guard with The Barbarian's knife....

With a quick motion, he tossed the weapon back to its owner.

THE BARBARIANS

That one was an easy choice, Geoffrey thought. Simply stealing—or was it recapturing?—a tankette and using it to drive away with Myka and The Barbarian didn't mean he had to go all the way to the barbarian lands with them. Let the guard revive and run to Dugald with the news. All Geoffrey had to do was to remove himself a few miles, find shelter, and bide his time.

One recaptured barbarian tankette might not even be missed. And the guard might not be believed—well, that was a thin hope—but, in any case, no one had any reason to suspect The Barbarian was still alive. There'd be no general pursuit.

Well ... maybe not. There was a man-at-arms choked to death, by a stronger arm than Geoffrey's, and it was The Barbarian's woman who would be missing. There might be quite a buzz about that.

Geoffrey shook his head in impatient annoyance. This kind of life demanded a great deal more thinking than he was accustomed to. All these unpredictable factors made a man's head spin.

And then again, maybe they didn't. The thing to do was to act, to do what would get him out of here now, and leave him free tomorrow to do whatever thinking tomorrow demanded. With a little practice, too, thinking would undoubtedly come more easily.

"All right," he said decisively, "let's get moving over in that direction, and see if the guards haven't gotten a little careless." He motioned to Myka and The Barbarian, and began to lead the way into the underbrush. He thrust out a hand to pull a sapling aside, and almost ran full-tilt into Harolde Dugald.

Dugald was almost exactly Geoffrey's age and size, but he had something Geoffrey lacked—a thin-lipped look of wolfish wisdom. His dark eyes were habitually slitted, and his mouth oddly off-center, always poised between a mirthless grin and a snarl. His long black hair curled under at the base of his skull, and his hands were covered

18

with heavy gold and silver rings. There was one for each finger and thumb, and all of them were set with knobby precious stones.

His lips parted now, and his long white teeth showed plainly in the semi-darkness. "I was coming back to inspect my prizes," he said in a voice like a fine-bladed saw chuckling through soft metal. "And look what I've found." The open mouth of his heavy, handmade side pistol pointed steadily between Geoffrey's eyes. "I find my erstwhile neighbor risen from the dead, and in the company of a crippled enemy and his leman. Indeed, my day is complete."

The one thing Geoffrey was not feeling was fear. The wire-thin strand of his accumulated rage was stretched to breaking. Somewhere, far from the forefront of his mind, he was feeling surprise and disappointment. He was perfectly aware of Dugald's weapon, and of what it would do to his head at this range. But Geoffrey was not stopping to think. And Dugald was a bit closer to him than he ought to have been.

Geoffrey's hands seemed to leap out. One tore the pistol out of Dugald's hand and knocked it spinning. The other cracked, open-palmed, against the other man's face, hard enough to split flesh and start the blood trickling down Dugald's cheek. The force of the combined blows sent Dugald staggering. He fell back, crashing into a bush, and hung against it. Stark fear shone in his eyes. He screamed: "Dugald! *Dugald!* To me! To me!"

For a second, everything went silent; nobles quarreling, guards roistering among the captures—suddenly the battlefield was still. Then the reaction to the rallying cry set off an entirely different kind of hubbub. The sound now was that of an alerted pack of dogs.

Once more, Geoffrey swept his hand across Dugald's face, feeling his own skin break over the knuckles. But there was no time for anything else. Now they had to run, and not in silence. Now everything went by the board, and the nearest safety was the best. Behind them as they tore through the brush, they could hear Dugald shouting:

"That way! The Barbarian's with him!" The Barbarian was grunting with every step. Myka was panting. Geoffrey was in the lead, his throat burning with every breath, not knowing where he was leading them, but trying to skirt around the pack of nobles that would be running toward them in the darkness.

He crashed against plated metal. He peered at it in the absolute darkness this far from the fires and torches. "Tankette!" he said hoarsely. "Empty." They scrambled onto it, Geoffrey pulling at The Barbarian's arm. "Down, Myka—inside. Ought to be room between steering posts and motor." He pushed the woman down through the hatch, and dropped back to the ground. He ran to the crank clipped to one track housing and thrust it into place. "You—you'll have to hang onto—turret," he panted to The Barbarian. "Help me start." He wound furiously at the starting crank until he felt the flywheel spin free of the ratchet, and then engaged the driveshaft. The tankette shuddered to the sudden torque. The motor resisted, turned its shaft reluctantly, spun the magneto, ignited, stuttered, coughed, and began to roar. The headlights flickered yellowly, glowed up to brightness as the engine built up revolutions. The Barbarian, clinging to the turret with one arm, pushed the choke control back to halfway and advanced the spark. Geoffrey scrambled up the sharply pitched rear deck, clawing for handholds on the radiator tubing, and dropped into the turret seat. He took the controls, kicked at the left side track control without caring, for the moment, whether Myka was in the way or not, spun the tankette halfway round, and pulled the throttle out as far as it would go. Its engine clamoring, its rigid tracks transmitting every shock and battering them, the tankette flogged forward through the brush. There was gunfire booming behind them, and there were other motors sputtering into life.

There was no one among the nobles to drive as well as Geoffrey could—certainly no one who could keep up with him at night, in country he knew. He could probably depend on that much.

He lit the carbide lamp over the panel.

Geoffrey looked at the crest worked into the metal, and laughed. He had even managed to steal Dugald's tankette.

*

By morning, they were a good fifty miles away from where the battle had been fought. They were almost as far as the Delaware River, and the ground was broken into low hills, each a little higher than the last. Geoffrey had only been this far away from his home a few times, before his father's death, and then never in this direction. Civilization was not considered to extend this far inland. When a young man went on his travels, preparatory for the day when he inherited his father's holdings and settled down to maintain them, he went along the coast, perhaps as far as Philadelphia or Hartford.

Geoffrey had always had a lively interest in strange surroundings. He had regretted the day his journeyings came to an end—not that he hadn't regretted his father's passing even more. Now, as dawn came up behind them, he could not help turning his head from side to side and looking at the strangely humped land, seeing for the first time a horizon which was not flat. He found himself intrigued by the thought that he had no way of knowing what lay beyond the next hill—that he would have to travel, and keep traveling, to satisfy a perpetually renewed curiosity.

All this occupied one part of his mind. Simultaneously, he wondered how much farther they'd travel in this vehicle. The huge sixteen-cylinder in-line engine was by now delivering about one-fourth of its rated fifty horsepower, with a good half of its spark plugs hopelessly fouled and the carburetor choked by the dust of yesterday's battle.

They were very low on shot and powder charges for the two-pounder turret cannon, as well. The tankette had of course never been serviced after the battle. There was one good thing—neither had their pursuers'. Looking back, Geoffrey could see no sign of them. But he could also see the plain imprint of the tankette's steel cleats stretched out behind them in a betraying line. The rigid, unsprung track left its mark on hard stone as easily as it did in soft earth. The wonder was that the tracks had not quite worn themselves out as yet, though all the rivets were badly strained and the tankette sounded like a barrel of stones tumbling downhill.

The Barbarian had spent the night with one arm thrown over the cannon barrel and the fingers of his other hand hooked over the edge of the turret hatch. In spite of the tankette's vicious jouncing, he had not moved or changed his position. Now he raised one hand to comb the shaggy hair away from his forehead, and there were faint bloody marks on the hatch.

"How much farther until we're over the mountains?" Geoffrey asked him.

"Over the—lad, we haven't even come to the beginning of them yet."

Geoffrey grimaced. "Then we'll never make it. Not in this vehicle."

"I didn't expect to. We'll walk until we reach the pass. I've got a support camp set up there."

"Walk? This is impossible country for people on foot. There are intransigent tribesmen all through this territory."

"How do you know?"

"How do I *know*? Why, everybody knows about them!"

The Barbarian looked at him thoughtfully, and with just the faintest trace of amusement. "Well, if *everybody* knows they're intransigent, I guess they are. I guess we'll just have to hope they don't spot us."

Geoffrey was a little nettled by The Barbarian's manner. It wasn't, after all, as if anybody claimed there were dragons or monsters or any other such oceanic thing living here. This was good, solid fact—people had actually come up here, tried to bring civilization to the tribes, and failed completely. They were, by all reports, hairy, dirty people equipped with accurate rifles. No one had bothered to press the issue, because obviously it was hardly worth it. Geoffrey had expected to have trouble with them—but he had expected to meet it in an armored vehicle. But now that the mountains had turned out to be so far away, the situation might grow quite serious. And The Barbarian didn't seem to care very much.

"Well, now, lad," he was saying, "if the tribesmen're that bad, maybe your friends the nobles won't dare follow us up here."

"They'll follow us," Geoffrey answered flatly. "I slapped Dugald's face."

"Oh. Oh, I didn't understand that. Code of honor—that sort of thing. All the civilized appurtenances."

"It's hardly funny."

"No, I suppose not. I don't suppose it occurred to you to kill him on the spot?"

"Kill a *noble* in hot blood?"

"Sorry. Code of honor again. Forget I mentioned it."

Geoffrey rankled under The Barbarian's barely concealed amusement. To avoid any more of this kind of thing, he pointedly turned and looked at the terrain behind them—something he ought to have done a little earlier. Three tankettes were in sight, only a few miles behind them, laboring down the slope of a hill.

And at that moment, as though rivetted iron had a dramatic sense of its own, their tankette coughed, spun lazily on one track as the crankshaft paused with a cam squarely between positions, and burned up the last drops of oil and alcohol in its fuel tank.

Geoffrey and Myka crouched down in a brushy hollow. The Barbarian had crawled up to the lip of the depression, and was peering through a clump of weeds at the oncoming trio. "That seems to be all of them," he said with a turn of his head. "It's possible they kept their speed down and nursed themselves along to save fuel. They might even have a fuel waggon coming up behind them. That's the way I'd do it. It would mean these three are all we can expect for a few hours, anyway, but that they'll be heavily reinforced some time later."

"That will hardly matter," Geoffrey muttered. Myka had found Dugald's personal rifle inside the tankette. Geoffrey was rolling cartridges quickly and expertly, using torn up charges from the turret cannon. He had made the choice between a round or two for the now immobile heavy weapon and a plentiful supply for the rifle, and would have been greatly surprised at anyone's choosing differently. The Barbarian had not even questioned it, and Myka was skillfully casting bullets with the help of the hissing alcohol stove and the bullet mold included in the rifle kit. There was plenty of finely ground priming powder, and even though Geoffrey was neither weighing the charges of cannon powder nor measuring the diameter of the cartridges he was rolling, no young noble of any pretensions whatsoever could not have done the same.

The rub lay in the fact that none of this was liable to do them much good. If they were to flee through the woods, there would certainly be time for only a shot or two when the tribesmen found them. If the rifle was to be used against the three nobles, then it was necessary, in all decency, to wait until the nobles had stopped, climbed out of their tankettes, equipped themselves equally, and a mutual ground of battle had been agreed upon. In that case, three against one would make short work of it.

The better chance lay with the woods and the tribesmen. It was the better chance, but Geoffrey did not relish it. He scowled as he dropped a primer charge down the rifle's barrel, followed it with a cartridge, took a cooled bullet from Myka, and tamped it down with the ramrod until it was firmly gripped by the collar on the cartridge. He took a square of clean flannel from its compartment in the butt and carefully wiped the lenses of the telescopic sight.

"Can I stop now?" Myka asked.

Geoffrey looked at her sharply. It had never occurred to him that the woman might simply be humoring him, and yet that was the tone her voice had taken. Truth to tell, he had simply handed her the stove, pig lead, and mold, and told her to go to work.

He looked at her now, remembering that he'd been hurried and possibly brusque. It ought not to matter—though it did—since she was hardly a lady entitled to courtesy. She hardly looked like anything, after hours crouched inside the tankette.

Her copper hair was smeared with grease, disarranged, and even singed where she had presumably leaned against a hot fitting. Her clothes were indescribably dirty and limp with perspiration. She was quite pale, and seemed to be fighting nausea—hardly surprising, with the exhaust fumes that must have been present in the compartment.

Nevertheless, her hair glinted where the sun struck it, and her litheness was only accented by the wrinkled clothing. Over-accented,

THE BARBARIANS

Geoffrey thought to himself as he looked at the length of limb revealed by her short trousers.

He flushed. "Of course. Thank you." He looked at the pile of finished bullets. There were enough of them to stand off an army, provided only the army did not shift about behind rocks and trees as the tribesmen did, or was not equally armed, as the nobles would be. Yet, a man had to try to the end. "You don't expect this to do much good," he said to the woman.

Myka grinned at him. "Do you?"

"No, frankly. But why did you help me?"

"To keep you busy."

"I see." He didn't. He scooped the bullets up, put them in one pocket, and dropped the cartridges in another. He stood up.

"There wasn't any point in letting you get nervous," Myka explained. "You can be quite a deadly boy in action, if what I've seen and heard about you is any indication. I didn't want you killing any of our friends." She was smiling at him without any malice whatsoever; rather, with a definite degree of fondness. Geoffrey did not even feel resentful at this business of being casually managed, as though he were liable to do something foolish.

But he scrambled up to a place beside The Barbarian in a burst of tense movement, and looked out toward the approaching tankettes. What Myka had just said to him, and the cryptic smile on The Barbarian's face, and a thought of Geoffrey's own, had all fitted themselves together in his mind.

There was no reason, really, to believe that barbarians would be hostile to barbarians, and certainly the inland raiders could not have returned year after year without *some* means of handling the mountain tribes. Friendship, or at least an alliance, would be the easiest way.

ALGIS BUDRYS

And out on the slope of the nearest hill, bearded men in homespun clothing were rolling boulders down on the advancing tankettes.

The slope of the hill was quite steep, and the boulders were massive. They tumbled and bounded with a speed that must have seemed terrifying from below. Tearing great chunks out of the earth, they rumbled down on the tankettes while the tribesmen yelled with bloodcurdling ferocity and fired on the tankettes with impossible rapidity. With respectable marksmanship, too. The nobles were swerving their vehicles frantically from side to side, trying to avoid the boulders, but their ability to do so was being destroyed by bullets that ricocheted viciously off the canted forepeak plating. All three of them were blundering about like cattle attacked by stinging insects. Only the lead tankette was still under anything like intelligent control. It lurched away from three boulders in succession, swinging on its treads and continuing to churn its way up the hillside.

Geoffrey saw the other two tankettes struck almost simultaneously. One took a boulder squarely between its tracks, and stopped in a shower of rock fragments. The track cleats bit futilely at the ground. The vehicle stalled, the boulder jammed against it. The impact did not seem to have been particularly severe; but the entire body of the tankette had been buckled and accordioned. Possibly only the boulder's own bulk between the tracks had kept them from coming together like the knees of a gored ox. It was impossible to tell where, in that crushed bulk, the turret and its occupant might be.

The other tankette took its boulder squarely in the flank. It began to roll over immediately, hurtling back down the hill, its driver half in and half out of its turret at the beginning of the first roll. Tankette and boulder came to rest together at the bottom of the hill, the stone nosing up against the metal.

THE BARBARIANS

Geoffrey looked at the scene with cold fury. "That's no fitting way for a noble to die!"

The Barbarian, who was sprawled out and watching calmly, nodded his head. "Probably not," he said dispassionately. "But that other man's giving a good account of himself."

The remaining tankette was almost in among the tribesmen. It had passed the point where a rolling boulder's momentum would be great enough to do much damage. As Geoffrey watched, the man in the turret yanked his lanyard, and a solid shot boomed through the straggled line of bearded men. If it had been grape or canister, it might have done a good deal of damage. But the cannon had been loaded with Geoffrey's tankette in mind, and the tribesmen only jeered. One of them dashed forward, under the cannon's smoking muzzle, and jammed a wedge-shaped stone between the left side track and the massive forward track roller. The track jammed, broke, and whipped back in whistling fragments. The tankette slewed around while the unharmed tribesman danced out of the way. The noble in the turret could only watch helplessly. Apparently he had no sidearm. Geoffrey peered at him as the tribesmen swarmed over the tankette and dragged him out of the turret. It was Dugald, and Geoffrey's arm still tingled from the slap that had knocked the pistol irretrievably into the night-shadowed brush at the battlefield.

"What are they going to do to him?" he asked The Barbarian.

"Make him meet the test of fitness, I suppose."

"Fitness?"

Geoffrey did not get the answer to his question immediately. The woods all around him were stirring, and bearded men in homespun, carrying fantastic rifles, were casually walking toward him. The Barbarian pushed himself up to his feet without any show of surprise.

"Howdy," he said. "Figured you were right around."

ALGIS BUDRYS

One of the tribesmen—a gaunt, incredibly tall man with a grizzled beard—nodded. "I seen you makin' signs while you was hangin' off that tank, before. Got a mark?"

The Barbarian extended his right arm and turned his wrist over. A faint double scar, crossed at right angles, showed in the skin.

The tribesman peered at it and grunted. "Old one."

"I got it twenty years ago, when I first came through here," The Barbarian answered.

"Double, too. Ain't many of those."

"My name's Hodd Savage."

"Oh," the tribesman said. His entire manner changed. Without becoming servile, it was respectful. He extended his hand. "Sime Weatherby." He and The Barbarian clasped hands. "That your woman down there?" the tribesman asked, nodding toward Myka.

"That's right."

"Good enough." For the first time, Weatherby looked directly at Geoffrey. "What about him?"

The Barbarian shook his head. "No mark."

The tribesman nodded. "I figured, from the way he was actin'." He seemed to make no particular signal—perhaps none was needed—but Geoffrey's arms were suddenly taken from behind, and his wrists were tied.

"We'll see if he can get him a mark today," Weatherby said. He looked to his left, where other men were just pushing Dugald into the ring they had formed around the group. "Seein' as there's two of them, one of 'em ought to make it."

Geoffrey and Dugald stared expressionlessly at each other. The Barbarian kept his eyes on Geoffrey's face. "That's right," he said. "Can't have two men fight to the death without one of them coming out alive, usually."

29

THE BARBARIANS

*

The tribesmen lived in wooden cabins tucked away among trees and hidden in narrow little valleys. Geoffrey was surprised to see windmills, and wire fencing for the cattle pastures that adjoined their homes. He was even more interested in their rifles, which, the tribesmen told him, were repeaters. He was puzzled by the absence of a cylinder, such as could be found on the generally unreliable revolvers one saw occasionally.

The tribesmen were treating both him and Dugald with a complete absence of the savagery he expected. They were being perfectly matter-of-fact. If his hands had not been tied, Geoffrey might not have been a prisoner at all. This puzzled him as well. A prisoner, after all, could not expect to be treated very well. True, he and Dugald were nobles, but this could not possibly mean anything to persons as uncivilized as mountain tribesmen.

Yet somehow, the only thing that was done was that all of them; the tribesmen, The Barbarian, Myka, Dugald and he—made their way to Weatherby's home. A number of the tribesmen continued on their way from there, going to their own homes to bring their families to watch the test. The remainder stayed behind to post guard. Dugald was put in one room, and Geoffrey in another. The Barbarian and Myka went off somewhere with Weatherby—presumably to have breakfast. Geoffrey could smell food cooking, somewhere toward the back of the house. The smell sat intolerably on his empty stomach.

He sat for perhaps a half hour in the room, which was almost bare of furniture. There was a straight-backed chair, in which he sat, a narrow bed, and a bureau. Even though his hands were still tied behind his back, he did his best to search the room for something to help him—though he had no idea of what he would do next after he managed to escape from the room itself.

The problem did not arise, because the room had been stripped of anything with a sharp edge on which to cut his lashings, and of anything else he might put to use. These people had obviously held prisoners here before. He sat back down in his chair, and stared at the wall.

Eventually, someone opened the door. Geoffrey looked over, and saw that it was The Barbarian. He looked at the inlander coldly, but The Barbarian did not seem to notice. He sat down on the edge of the bed.

"On top of everything else," he began without preamble, "I've just finished a hearty breakfast. That ought to really make you mad at me."

"I'm not concerned with you, or your meals," Geoffrey pointed out.

The Barbarian's eyes twinkled. "It doesn't bother you, my getting your help and then not protecting you from these intransigent tribesmen?"

"Hardly. I'd be a fool to expect it."

"Would you, now? Look, bucko—these people live a hard way of life. Living on a mountain is a good way not to live comfortably. But it's a good way of living your own way, *if* you can stand the gaff. These people can. Every one of them. They've got their marks to prove it. Every last one of them has fought it out face to face with another man, and proved his fitness to take up space in this territory. See—it's a social code. And they'll extend it to cover any stranger who doesn't get killed on his way here. If you can get your mark, you're welcome here for the rest of your life. They keep their clan stock fresh and vigorous that way. And it all has the virtue of being a uniform, just, rigid code that covers every man in the group. These barbarian cultures aren't ever happy without a good code to their name, you know."

31

THE BARBARIANS

"Yours seems to lack one."

The Barbarian chuckled. "Oh, no. We've got one, all right, or you'd never have had me to worry you. Nothing we like better than a good, talented enemy. You know, these people here in the mountains used to be our favorite enemies. But so many of us wound up getting our marks, it just got to be futile. Once you're in, you know, you're a full-fledged clan member. That sort of divided our loyalties. The problem just seemed to solve itself, though. We understand them, they understand us, we trade back and forth ... hell, it's all one family."

Geoffrey frowned. "You mean—they got those rifles from you?"

"Sure. We're full of ingenuity—for barbarians, that is. Not in the same class with you seaboard nobles, of course, but we poke along." The Barbarian stood up, and his expression turned serious. "Look, son—you remember that knife of mine you borrowed for a while? I'll have to lend it to you again, in about twenty minutes. Your friend Dugald's going to have one just like it, and your left arms are going to be tied together at the wrists. I hope you remember what I happened to tell you about how to use it, because under the rules of the code, I'm not allowed to instruct you."

And Geoffrey was left alone.

*

There was a hard-packed area of dirt in front of Weatherby's home, and now its edges were crowded with tribesmen, many of whom had brought their women and children. Weatherby, together with a spare, capable-looking woman, and with The Barbarian and Myka, sat on his porch. One of the tribesmen was wrapping Geoffrey's and Dugald's forearms together. Geoffrey watched him with complete detachment. He stole a glance over toward Weatherby's porch, and it seemed to him that Myka was tense and anxious. He couldn't be sure....

ALGIS BUDRYS

The fingers of his right hand gripped the haft of The Barbarian's knife. He held it with his thumb along the blade, knowing that if he drew his arm up, to stab downward, or back, to slash, Dugald would have a perfect opening. It was his thought, remembering that razor-keen blade, that he ought to be able to do plenty of damage with a simple underhand twist of his arm. He did not look down to see how Dugald was holding the knife he'd been given. That would have been unfair.

The crowd of watching tribesmen was completely silent. This was a serious business with them, Geoffrey reflected.

The tribesman tying their wrists had finished the job. He stepped back. "Anytime after I say 'Go,' you boys set to it. Anything goes and dead man loses. If you don't fight, we kill you both."

For the first time since their capture, Geoffrey looked squarely into Dugald's slit eyes. "I'm sorry we have to do this to each other in this way, Dugald," he said.

"Go!" the tribesman shouted, and jumped back.

Dugald spat at Geoffrey's face. Geoffrey twitched his head involuntarily, realized what he'd done, and threw himself off his feet, pulling Dugald with him and just escaping the downward arc of Dugald's plunging knife. The momentum of Dugald's swing, combined with Geoffrey's weight, pulled him completely over Geoffrey's shoulder. The two of them jerked abruptly flat on the ground, their shoulders wrenched, sprawled out facing each other and tied together like two cats on a string.

The crowd shouted.

Geoffrey had landed full on his ribs, and for a moment he saw nothing but a red mist. Then his eyes cleared and he was staring into Dugald's face. Dugald snarled at him, and pawed out with his knife, at the advantage now because he could stab downward. Geoffrey rolled, and Dugald perforce rolled with him. The stab missed again, and Geoffrey, on his back, jabbed blindly over his head and reached nothing. Then they were on their stomachs again.

Dugald was panting, his face running wet. The long black hair was full of dust, and his face was smeared. If ever Geoffrey had seen a man in an animal state, that was what Dugald resembled. Geoffrey thought wildly; Is this what a *noble* is?

"I'll kill you!" Dugald bayed at him, and Geoffrey's hackles rose. This is not a man, he thought. This is nothing that deserves to live.

Dugald's arm snapped back, knife poised, and drove downward again. Geoffrey suddenly coiled his back muscles and heaved on his left arm, yanking himself up against Dugald's chest. He snapped his hips sideward, and Dugald's knife missed him completely for the third and fatal time. The Barbarian's knife slipped upward into Dugald's rib cage, and suddenly Geoffrey was drenched with blood. Dugald's teeth bit into his neck, but the other man's jaws were already slackening. Geoffrey let himself slump, and hoped they would cut this carrion away from him as soon as possible. He heard the crowd yelping, and felt The Barbarian plucking the knife out of his hand. His arm was freed, and he rolled away.

"By God, I *knew* you had the stuff," The Barbarian was booming. "I knew they had to start breeding men out on the coast sooner or later. Here—give me your other wrist." The blade burned his skin twice each way—once for victory and once for special aptitude—and then Myka pressed a cloth to the wound.

She was shaking her head. "I've never seen it done better. You're a natural born fighter, lad. I've got one of my sisters all picked out for you."

Geoffrey smiled up at The Barbarian, a little ruefully. "It seems you and I'll be going back to the coast together, next year."

"Had it in mind all along, lad," The Barbarian said. "If I can't lick 'em, I'll be damned if I won't make 'em join me."

"It's an effective system," Geoffrey said.

"That it is, lad. That it is. And now, if you'll climb up to your feet, let's go get you some breakfast."

www.ingramcontent.com/pod-product-compliance
Lightning Source LLC
Chambersburg PA
CBHW020348130626
46549CB00003B/1354